Tasty Baby Belly Buttons

by Judy Sierra   illustrated by Meilo So

Alfred A. Knopf   New York

In Japan, long ago, many towns and villages were terrorized by a gang of oni. These oni were great hulking monsters. Some had red faces and some had green faces. They all had sharp teeth and horns on their heads, and they wore no clothes except the skins of tigers, which they wrapped tightly around their hips. The oni lived on an island called Onigashima, and from time to time they would leave their castle and travel around Japan kidnapping children in order to find their favorite treat—belly buttons.

In one village lived an old woman and an old man who had no children.

"If only I had a child," sighed the old woman, "I would teach her how to cook the best millet dumplings in Japan." The old woman was a very good cook.

"If only I had a child," said the old man, "I could teach him to protect people who are weak and helpless." In his youth, the man had been a warrior.

One morning, as the old woman was washing clothes in the river, a melon came floating along, *tsunbara, tsunbara.* She waded into the water and nudged the melon toward her until she could lift it. Then she carried it to the field where her husband was working.

The old man was delighted to see the melon, for he was hungry and thirsty. He was just getting ready to cut it open when he heard a crying noise, *boro, boro,* coming from inside.

He and his wife pulled the melon open with their hands,
and in the center they beheld a tiny, perfect baby girl. They
named her Uriko-hime—"melon princess."

Uriko grew more quickly than other children, and by the time she was five years old she was cooking millet dumplings with her mother and learning sword fighting from her father.

One day, everyone in the village heard an awful sound. A troop of oni came tromping into town, *zushin, zushin*. They grabbed all the little babies they could find and put them into their cart, and no one dared stop them because they were so big and so strong. As they wheeled the cart away, they shouted,

"Belly buttons,
Belly buttons,
Tasty baby belly buttons!"

But the oni did not take Uriko. Perhaps this was because she was born from a melon and did not have a belly button.

Uriko was furious at what the oni had done. "Father, make me a sword," she commanded. "Mother, help me cook a big batch of millet dumplings. I am going to Onigashima to rescue the babies."

Her parents were afraid for their little daughter, but at last they agreed that she could go, so long as she took the dog with her. The next morning, Uriko set out, wearing a shiny new sword at her side and carrying a heavy sack of millet dumplings on her back. She and the dog marched along the path together, *tontoko, tontoko.*

Suddenly, they heard a terrific whirring sound. A pheasant flew down and blocked their way, calling,

"*Ken, ken,*

Ken, ken,

I smell millet dumplings."

"We are going to Onigashima to rescue the babies," said Uriko, "and we could use a brave companion. If you will join us, we will share our dumplings with you." She tossed a dumpling to the bird, who swallowed it in one gulp.

"Yes," said the pheasant. "I will join you."

And so Uriko and the dog and the pheasant marched along the path, *tontoko, tontoko.*

They entered a dark forest. A monkey swung down from the trees and blocked their way, showing his sharp teeth and chattering,

"*Kya, kya,*

Kya, kya,

I smell millet dumplings."

"We are on our way to Onigashima to rescue the babies," said Uriko, "and if you will come with us, we will share our millet dumplings with you." She tossed a dumpling to the monkey, and he ate it greedily.

"Wonderful!" he cried. "This millet dumpling makes me feel stronger than ten monkeys. Let's go!"

Soon they reached the seaside, where they found a boat and sailed to the rocky shore of Onigashima. They saw a castle on a cliff high above them, and in the distance they could hear

"Belly buttons,
Belly buttons,
Tasty baby belly buttons!"

The four companions followed a steep path to the top of the cliff. They walked boldly up to the castle gate and knocked, *don, don*. The door creaked open, and they looked up at the hairy knees, the huge belly, the green face, and the sharp horns of the chief oni. But the girl and the dog and the pheasant and the monkey were so small that the chief oni did not see them at all. Quickly, they ran between his legs and were inside the castle.

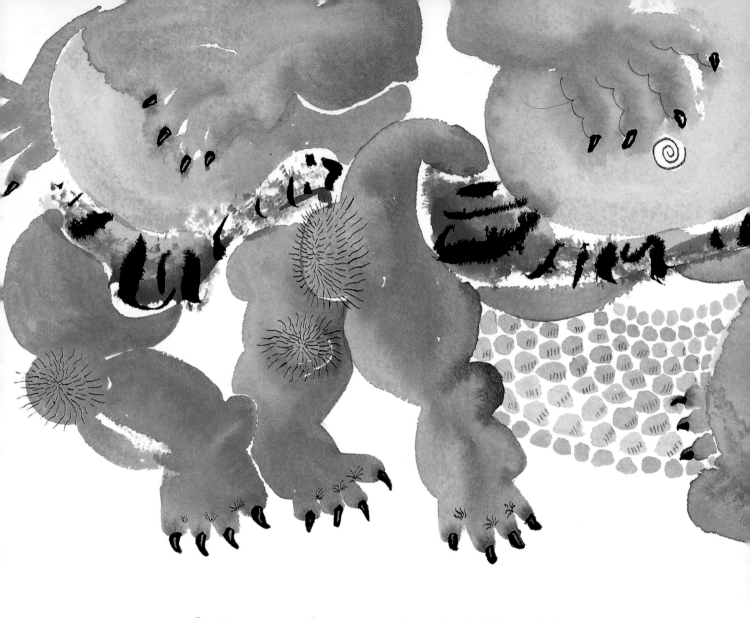

In the center of a courtyard sat the babies, all tied
up together, crying so sadly, *boro, boro, boro, boro.*
Three green oni and three red oni danced around
the babies, singing,

"Belly buttons,
Belly buttons,
Tasty baby belly buttons!"

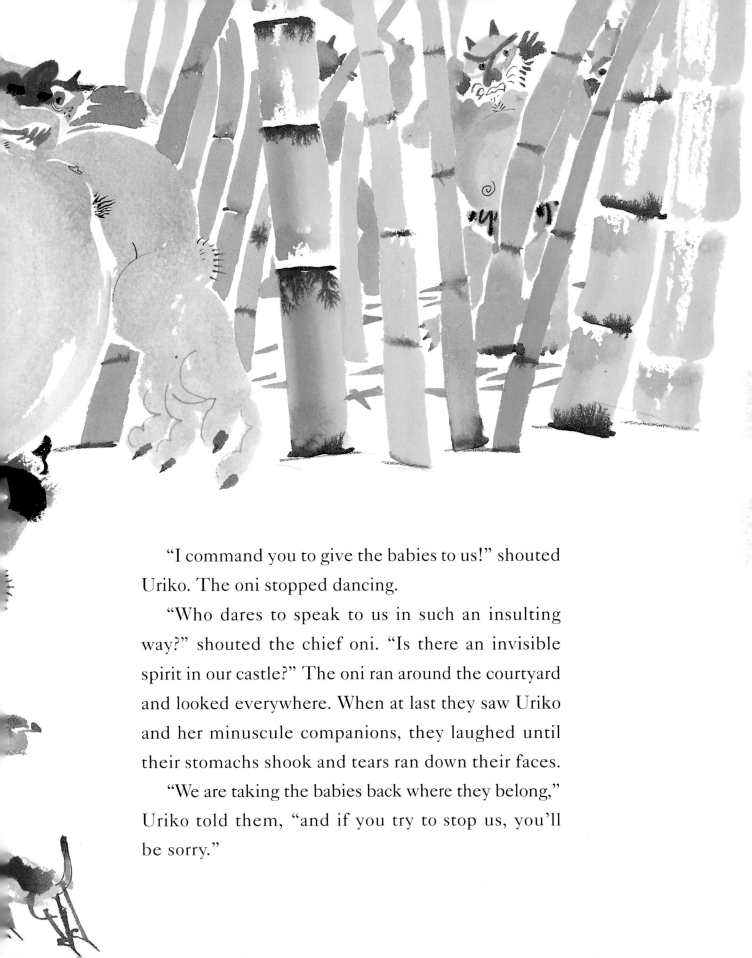

"I command you to give the babies to us!" shouted Uriko. The oni stopped dancing.

"Who dares to speak to us in such an insulting way?" shouted the chief oni. "Is there an invisible spirit in our castle?" The oni ran around the courtyard and looked everywhere. When at last they saw Uriko and her minuscule companions, they laughed until their stomachs shook and tears ran down their faces.

"We are taking the babies back where they belong," Uriko told them, "and if you try to stop us, you'll be sorry."

The oni grabbed their clubs. "We will crush you like ants!" they roared. "Charge, my fearless fighters!" cried Uriko, and she rushed to guard the babies. The dog raced around the oni's feet and nipped their toes, and when they tried to bash him with their clubs, they smashed their own feet instead.

The monkey climbed up the oni's legs and bit their knees, and when they tried to knock him off, they smacked their own kneecaps instead.

The pheasant flew around and around the oni's heads and dived at their eyes, and when the oni tried to brush her away with their clubs, they bopped each other on the head and fell to the ground.

Uriko took her sword and cut the ropes that tied the babies. Then she lifted them onto the cart and gave each one a dumpling.

"You may live here on your island," she told the defeated oni, "but do not ever set foot in our country again."

"We won't, we promise, *boro, boro*," sobbed the oni. "Just go away and leave us alone, *boro, boro*."

Uriko had to give each of the oni a millet dumpling, too, so that they would stop crying.

The monkey and the pheasant searched the castle and found many bags of gold and other treasures that the oni had stolen, and they placed them on the cart, in between the babies. Then the four companions carefully guided the cart down to the shore. They crossed the ocean and hurried to Uriko's village.

Soon the babies were in the arms of their happy parents. Uriko gave the bags of gold and treasure to her own mother and father. They returned as much of it as they could to the people the oni had stolen it from, and shared the rest with the families in their village.

The monkey and the pheasant and the dog stayed with
Uriko in her house, and in the evening they would sit by the fire
and munch millet dumplings and tell and retell the story of
their adventure in Onigashima.

Author's Note

The story of the miraculous child who marches off to Onigashima to battle the oni is one of the best-known of Japan's folktales. Usually, the hero of the tale is Momotaro, a boy born from a peach. In Shimane prefecture, though, the tale has sometimes been told with a heroine—Uriko-hime (pronounced ooh-ree-koh-HEE-may, or OOH-ree-koh for short), the melon princess. This retelling is based on two orally collected tales that were first published in the Japanese folklore journal *Mukashibanashi kenkyu*. I have added details from similar folktales and from Japanese folk beliefs.

Oni are creatures of folklore, much like the ogres and giants of other cultures. According to oral tradition, oni had insatiable appetites for human navels and would kidnap people in order to get this delicacy. Even now, adults jokingly warn young children to cover their belly buttons, lest an oni come and munch them. Certain words in this story, such as *boro, boro* and *zushin, zushin*, are part of the vocabulary of traditional Japanese storytellers—like *fee-fi-fo-fum* in tales of English giants.

For Myrriah —J.S.

For Bobo, friend and gourmet —M.S.

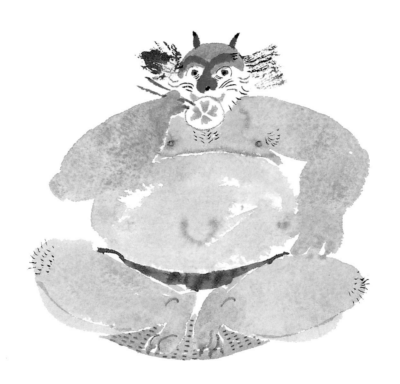

THIS IS A BORZOI BOOK PUBLISHED BY ALFRED A. KNOPF, INC.

Text copyright © 1999 by Judy Sierra. Illustrations copyright © 1999 by Meilo So.

All rights reserved under International and Pan-American Copyright Conventions.

Published in the United States of America by Alfred A. Knopf, Inc.,

and simultaneously in Canada by Random House of Canada Limited, Toronto.

Distributed by Random House, Inc., New York.

www.randomhouse.com/kids

Library of Congress Cataloging-in-Publication Data

Sierra, Judy.

Tasty baby belly buttons : a Japanese folktale / by Judy Sierra ; illustrated by Meilo So.

p. cm.

Summary: Uriko-hime, a girl born from a melon, battles the monstrous oni,

who steal babies to eat their tasty belly buttons.

ISBN 0-679-89369-5 (trade). — ISBN 0-679-99369-X (lib. bdg.)

[1. Folklore—Japan.] I. So, Meilo, ill. II. Title.

PZ8.1.S573Tas 1999

398.2'0952'01—dc21 98-22524

Printed in Hong Kong

10 9 8 7 6 5 4 3 2 1

First Edition